STILL

ON

EARTH

POEMS

STILL

ON

EARTH

David Romtvedt

LOUISIANA STATE UNIVERSITY PRESS
BATON ROUGE

Published by Louisiana State University Press
lsupress.org

LSU Press Paperback Original

DESIGNER: Michelle A. Neustrom
TYPEFACE: Whitman, text; Jost, display

COVER ILLUSTRATION: *Poppy Pods*, 2018, by Josie Mendelsohn.

LIBRARY OF CONGRESS CATALOGING-IN-PUBLICATION DATA

Names: Romtvedt, David, author.
Title: Still on Earth : poems / David Romtvedt.
Description: Baton Rouge : Louisiana State University Press, 2025.
Identifiers: LCCN 2024047663 (print) | LCCN 2024047664 (ebook) |
    ISBN 978-0-8071-8396-0 (paperback) | ISBN 978-0-8071-8447-9 (epub) |
    ISBN 978-0-8071-8448-6 (pdf)
Subjects: LCGFT: Poetry.
Classification: LCC PS3568.O5655 S75 2025 (print) | LCC PS3568.O5655 (ebook) |
    DDC 811/.54—dc23/eng/20241021
LC record available at https://lccn.loc.gov/2024047663
LC ebook record available at https://lccn.loc.gov/2024047664

CONTENTS

II. THE ANGEL

III. THE POET

ACKNOWLEDGMENTS

Thanks to the following publications where these poems first appeared:

American Poetry Review: "Counting Sheep"; *Atlanta Review:* "Tango Shmango" (as "Dilemmas of the Angels: Tango"); *Mantis:* "Job's Lawsuit" (as "Dilemmas of the Angels: Job's Lawsuit") and "Reading the Odyssey at the Kitchen Table" (as "Dilemmas of the Angels: Reading the Odyssey at the Kitchen Table"); *Nomad:* "Interstellar"; *Ploughshares:* "Running Away" and "Studying"; *Rattle:* "Watering the Trees"; *Screaming Sheep:* "Atomic Bomb" (as "Rocket in his Pocket"); *The Sun:* "Things to Do in Buffalo, Wyoming, While Waiting Out the Corona Virus."

"Election Night" (as "Election Night in Wyoming") and "Gettysburg" (as "Hearing the President Speak") appeared in *Not My President,* edited by Josh Gaines (2017).

"Western History" (as "National Politics in Yellowstone Park, July 29, 1914") appeared in the Academy of American Poets and National Endowment for the Arts America's National Parks project. It was published on Poets.org. Reprinted by permission of the Academy of American Poets, 75 Maiden Lane, Suite 901, New York, NY 10038.

Some of the previously published poems have been revised to such a degree that they might be seen as new poems. Still, I want to thank the editors who published the earlier versions—the springboards for the revised poems, which perhaps can be thought of as translations of their earlier selves. I'm deeply grateful to James W. Long, Neal Novak, and everyone at Louisiana State University Press for their support of my work. Thank you to the University of Wyoming MFA program, where many of the poems in this book were begun. For help with shaping the book, I want to thank Margo

Brown, who read, listened to, and commented on many drafts of the poems. And lastly, thank you to the anonymous outside reader who reviewed the manuscript for LSU Press and whose detailed, insightful comments led me to rethink and, I hope, improve both individual poems and the overall arc of the book.

I.

THE

PERSON

Interstellar

When I was a kid I wanted the aliens
to land, open the door of their ship
and appear, halo of light around their heads,
seven-fingered hands in silver gloves
waving me on board while speaking
some unknown language like French.

The years have passed
and the ship hasn't come.

I lean out the door and sniff the air,
cock my ear listening
for the UPS truck in the distance,
back-ordered package on its way.

When the truck stops, I lift my front paws
onto the steel step and leap up.
The driver leans down, biscuit in hand.

From the open doorway, I call out,
"Ne t'inquiètes pas—
je t'enverrais une postale,"
surprising everyone
with my knowledge of French.

Thunderstorm

The dark clouds hide the sun,
a flash of lightning and crack of thunder.

My father worries I'll be a candy-ass—
I'm already ten, time to toughen up.

It's the mother of all thunderstorms—
the windows rattling, doors banging.

He drags me to the tallest tree in the yard,
tells me not to move. I do, I'll be sorry.

The rain is pounding down, water running a river,
the jumpy feeling from electricity in the air.

I tell him I'm scared. "You wanta see scared?
I'll show you scared." Throws me into the storm.

Another crack, lightning slicing
toward the house, blinding wall of light.

I stand there, not moving, clothes heavy,
hair soaked, toughening up.

Baking Bread

In the kitchen
my father kneads dough,
shaping it in the early morning dark.

Bread must be beaten
to make it rise, nature being
an infinity of antagonisms.

Rolling the house out flat
and folding it over itself,
never mind who's inside.

Having greased the pans,
he tells me to check the oven,
make sure it's hot enough to bake.

Secrets

My father lifted me by the ear and threw me
to the floor, sending me for the special belt
he kept in his dresser. Hurrying, I yanked
the drawer open causing the miniature Christ
nailed to a cross of stained walnut and mounted
on a cherrywood pedestal to wobble. Belt
in hand I ran back to my father who bent me
over a chair and delivered the blows.

Summer nights, I'd lie in bed looking out
the window, imagining my mother leaning
over me, whispering, "Get up." She's put
my kid sister on a blanket in the back seat
of the car, her packed bag for a pillow.

I sit up front as we roll silently to the street.
Only then does she start the engine and drive
to the bus depot where she buys three tickets
to as far away as her money will take us.

Keys still hanging in the ignition, my father
dead, I wonder what secrets he might have told
that last summer day as he lay on the asphalt,
skin purpling in the heat, alone, tongue swollen
so that even had someone been there to listen,
he would have been unable to speak.

Studying

I figured if I studied enough, life would make sense
so I skipped the games and the girls, ate lunch
in a hurry, and spent the afternoons in the library.

On Saturday nights when everyone was out
gunning their engines, I camped alone at the beach
listening to the lap of waves and the chittering of birds.

Flashlight in hand, I read texts by long-dead writers
whose names I couldn't pronounce. Years passed.
I had my doubts, but let habit carry me.

They say the proximity of death causes
the trivial to fall away, revealing what matters.
I didn't feel that. I just liked studying.

It's like a long day's work—the oblique
afternoon light, the muscles in my arms
trembling, the sweat rolling down my face.

Running Away

I found a boat tied up
at the water's edge,
rocking, rope frayed, oars
banging in their locks.

At home, you never
knew what might
happen. A surprise
a minute, they say.

In the distance,
dark clouds, no trace
of the other shore.
It might have been

wise to have
brought a compass
and life jacket,
to have packed a lunch.

Counting Sheep

My mother said when my father took off
and she couldn't sleep she counted sheep.
No word where he went or when he'd return,
I too took to counting—Canada's provinces,
Mexico's states, Cajun fiddlers, Renaissance
painters, writers who'd committed suicide
and those who'd lived to a ripe-old age,
ripe fruit, corporate brands, rich and poor
countries, Academy Award–winning
supporting actors, national currencies.

I counted the War of Independence, the War
of 1812, the Mexican American War, the U.S.
Civil War, the Spanish American War, World
Wars I and II, Korea—a police action not a war,
but I counted it anyway—Vietnam, Grenada,
Panama, Haiti, Nicaragua, Biafra, Kosovo, South
Sudan, Chechnya, Afghanistan, Kurdistan, Iraq,
the Six-Day Arab-Israeli War, Ukraine.

I counted the war on drugs, and on poverty
and terror, the war to defeat cancer, eradicate
invasive plants on public lands, the Cold War,
the war on crime, the war between the sexes,
nuclear war, which made me think of counting
the things I fear, maybe just count the days
on the calendar. With that, I rolled over,
still counting, no telling when my father
might return, how much time I have left.

At the Stove

I wrap myself in my sweater
of fear, gloves and hat, wool socks,
winter coat, insulated boots.
They pinch but they're all I have.

Biking above town at dusk, winter
retreating into spring, a mountain lion
ran across the path hard behind a deer.
I could hear it breathe.

I dreamt I invented something to save us
but when I looked down, it was burning
a hole in the ground, small then bigger.

There are six thousand bison in Yellowstone.
This year eleven hundred walked across
the park boundary into Montana and were shot.
Once there were sixty million on the Great Plains.

I've jammed all the wood I can
into the stove, the fire blazing.
And still, I need another coat
over my sweater.

The Kite

Winter nears its end and the geese
come home to the still-frozen ponds,
dragging me behind them like the rag tail
of a kite, my childhood running down a hill.

Driving the long valley, I see the glow
of eyes at the side of the road,
animals hidden from sight, scruffle
in the brush as they turn to go.

I take my foot off the gas, and we come
to a stop. Engine still, the heater fan whirs
into silence. The headlight beams blink

as the car sinks into the snow. I lift the kite
from the back seat and step into the dark,
the ball of string unwinding from my hand.

Watering the Trees

Seeing the neighbor watering his pear tree,
I see my father watering the mulberries
in our yard. Bitter after his day of labor,
he turns away and I wait, imagining he will
speak across the years and space and what
passed between us will pass away. This
is how I live—pleased to hope in vain,
happy I'll never see my father again.

The neighbor starts yelling, face purple,
the veins in his neck ropes pulled tight.
Same veins in my father's neck. For him,
it was the bosses. For the neighbor, it's
the idiot liberals, every one of us. Funny
that he likes me. I like him. Maybe
we're changing the shape of the universe,
irony the literary equivalent of the worm-
hole that lets our rocket go faster than
the speed of light. Drop in and come out
a door that isn't there until you open it.

Falling Backwards

Sand warm beneath my feet, arms spread,
falling backwards into the water, the shock
of cold and flash of light, gulls skimming
the waves, grasshoppers rattling on the rocky
hillside, cattle coming down to drink. I'm
happy to be alive, happier with each day
that passes, childhood left behind for good.

I don't mean it was all bad. Those mornings
below freezing—rare in southern Arizona—
it was exciting to wear a coat, to find ice
in the gutter and shatter the glassy surface,
pick up a shard and look through it to see
school, floating there in the distance,
no longer tethered to the earth, life more
than I knew, the ice melting in my hand.

Me and the Pigs

"Brains to burn and you can't get a job,"
my father said, and "I never
had work I liked. You won't either."

But I had no trouble getting a job
and mostly liked my work.

One day, mucking out the barn on a small farm—
a few cows and pigs, chickens, a goat
that was half pet, and two dogs, both jealous
of the goat—the rendering truck showed up.

Humane death, the contract said,
and I guess it was true.
The pig wasn't on the ground
but a few minutes before being lifted
into the truck and hauled away.

The other pigs made a circle and stood
staring at the spot—ten, fifteen minutes.
Not so much waiting, I thought, as attending.

There before me the spot on the desert
where my father lay, not quite dead,
disappointment in his eyes.

I leaned my shovel on the fence
and stepped into the circle,
me and the pigs.

Long Haul

Pulling up to the house after a month
on the road, I sit, hands on the wheel,
watching the kids play in the street—
kick the can, streetlamp on the corner
home base, the narrow circle of light
within which one cannot be touched.

I step down, asphalt warm after the day's
heat, the desert in bloom. Here they
come, arms waving, words spilling
from their mouths, my son shouting,
"Aita, zer ekarri diguzu," showing off
in Basque, the tongue his grandparents
tell him we spoke before the Fall, before
we were thrown out of the Garden.

I hold up my hands pretending I've got
nothing when wham, the whole mob
slams into me and down we go, a little
dust devil spinning into darkness, kids
sitting on my back, pinning my arms
behind me. I resist, seeing my father
above me, arms raised to deliver a blow,
then relax, shouting at the kids, "You'll
never take me alive," all of us laughing.

State of the Union

At seven in the evening we sit down
before the television to await a report
on the progress of democracy.

The president blinks furiously.
I hold the arms of my chair so hard
that my fingers ache.

My wife comes in and turns the television off,
says, "It's your childhood," then asks me
to come to bed before it's too late.

Election Night

The smell of sulfur dioxide
and ammonia from the paper mill,
kelp from the harbor, the future
knocking at my door, the doctor
calling to tell me I have cancer.
He's sorry. I know everyone
has to die. Still, I'm surprised.
The wind tugs at the screen door.
I latch it then go to the kitchen
to make hot chocolate while they
count the votes. At the window
snow is falling. He doesn't say
how long I have or how worried
I should be. Seated on the couch,
my mother and father listen
as the newscaster runs through
the numbers. Arms draped over
each other's shoulders, they look
happier than when they were alive,
happier than when I was a kid
and they sat on either side of me
in church holding my hands
so I couldn't wiggle or run away.
They slide apart and pat the couch,
inviting me to sit between them.
"I'll just check the door one more
time," I say, as the wind picks up,
"make sure it's really latched,"
before the outcome is announced.

Down from the Mountain

While the defenders die in Ukraine,
I take a mountain bike ride, the trail
through the trees and along the creek.
I'm not sure what else to do. Down
from the mountain I'm back on city
streets, the asphalt wet and dark,
mud flying off the bike's tires
and splattering the back of my coat.
At the light I pull up behind a pickup,
the silver silhouette of a buxom girl
on the rear window, diesel fumes,
a bumper sticker that says TRUMP
2024—the Revenge Tour. How about
PUTIN 2024—skip the middleman?
But cynical humor rarely gets us far.
My stomach turns as my heart leaps
from the cage of my chest, crouching
again under my desk, eight years old.
The teacher, the young and pretty one
who is tall and slouches, tells us
to pull our shirts over our heads
and cover our faces as even a thin
layer of cloth will keep our skin
from being peeled off by the blast.
Half-forgotten days, warnings and
fears, canned food and jugs of water
lined up along the bathroom wall,
the neighbor digging up his yard
to make a bomb shelter, sorry
he can't save us too, hauling dirt
away and dumping it on the desert
where the small animals burrow
and the coyotes hunt in darkness.

How foolish I was to believe in
time undisturbed, my shirt covering
my face, the light about to change.

Things to Do in Buffalo, Wyoming, While Waiting Out the Corona Virus

Chop wood, shovel snow, bake bread,
make dinner, and after, take the compost
to the bin, nearly full though only half
decomposed. Citrus is the worst, the rinds
of orange, lemon, grapefruit, and lime,
and also avocado, the skins and pits.
November before last, so long ago now,
I was in the garden, scraping the snow
off the beds, digging the compost
in before the ground froze. There
amid the remains of summer's mint
and parsley, potatoes and peas,
was a six-inch stalk, a plant I didn't know.
I lifted it from the cold earth, brushed
the snow away and saw it was avocado.
Yes, avocado, sprouted from an afternoon
of Guacamole and gin and tonics. I dug up
a little more of the soil, put that
and the unlikely avocado into a clay pot
and took it into the warm house, the wood
I'd chopped burning in the stove. I meant
this poem to be about the things we can do
trapped now in ourselves, wrapped up
against a virus writing letters and reading
novels, inventing dinners from frozen foods
and legumes soaked overnight, bundling up
in layers to lie on the ground and watch
the stars. Things like that. But it turns out
this poem's about compost, that is to say
about transformation, how we change
moving through the days, and the days,
how they change moving through us.

Admission

The nurse at the clinic scowled,
angry that I was wearing a mask.

Ours is a freedom-loving state
so I was used to it.

The doctor explained that masks
do nothing to stop the spread of disease.

I didn't take the time to argue
as it turns out my situation's serious.

It's not that I'm coy, just not sure
I can face the numbers, I mean the days.

In the news it was the usual.
No need to make a list.

My wife and I watched a romantic comedy.
My one regret, I joked—never to have slept with Sandra Bullock.

You can see how hard it is to keep things under control,
lines growing longer, things I've borrowed, notes coming due.

Spade in hand, my father bent over his iris bed,
sun darkening his skin, singing to himself.

Another doctor took off her mask and held me.
I could feel her heart beating against my own.

Still on Earth

It being Sunday, the factories
are quiet, the cars are resting
in garages or nestled against
the curbs along the street.

Off duty, the dogs stop barking,
the wild turkeys cross the road
without looking, and the lake
pretends to be a sheet of glass.

I wrote of another Sunday—
night, machines off, lights out,
what I saw as the endurance
of beauty in the face of time.

Now here's my daughter,
a grown woman and a child
of six, riding her bike alone
for the first time, up and down
the alley, never mind the mud,
never mind the rain threatening
to fall as it has for days.

On the bike's handlebars
I've mounted a chrome bell
which my daughter rings
as she rides, the air retreating
before her. And look, here
I am, ringing the same bell,
time retreating before me.

Real Money

After my father's death, I'd see him now and again
disappearing around a corner like when he was alive.
No wave, no goodbye, gone then back, still no word
about where he'd been, what he'd done, a little cash
in his pockets, handing it over to my mother.

Or I'd see him getting on the bus on his way to work—
the paper mill, later the aluminum extrusion plant.
Different towns, same seat, face pressed to the window.

He was at the kitchen table after supper leaning over
the paper, sounding out the words. Finished, he lay
before the television, feet twitching, eyelids fluttering.
If you didn't know him, you'd think he was asleep.

Once I saw him at the supermarket. That was odd
as my mother did the shopping, but there he was
lifting canned beans and frozen peas onto the counter,
telling the clerk a loud and vulgar joke hoping no one
would notice he was paying with food stamps not
real money, real money being what he worried about
every day and what I've worried about, too, standing
beside him, the both of us trying to pay our way.

Only Words

Night and the desert cools off
enough to sit outside watching the moon,
the house empty, the dusty air still,
the clouds' promise of rain unfulfilled.

My father hated funerals, the unwinding
of the days. Morbid, he said, and refused
to attend even his own, asking to be
cremated, ashes tossed to the wind.

The moon falls toward the horizon,
my father's unblinking eye looking down
from Heaven or up from Hell, gate closed.

Go, I think, and good riddance but say
nothing, feeling words aren't always
cathartic. Sometimes they're only words.

No Religion at All

I summarize Buddhism for a group
of visiting Catholics—the Four Noble Truths,
the Eight-Fold Path, the Middle Way.

"Why, that's no religion at all," a man
says, then apologizes. "It's okay,"
I say, "I know what you mean."

A friend died and after the service
I stood in the rectory
eating store-bought cake.

I really believed my friend
would live forever. I would, too.
Never mind the evidence.

Zen students now and again nod off
and fall from their cushions, cracking
their heads on the wooden floor.

Terrible cake, a plastic fork,
and a paper plate.
I had a second piece.

When the students come around,
I tell them it's natural to feel drowsy,
and add, if you fall asleep

but stay upright, you're still sitting.
As I'm the master, several of them
take me seriously.

II.

THE

ANGEL

First Day

Say you're an angel newly fallen to earth,
sunlight silver across the corniced ridgeline,
fresh snow covering old, chickadee calling
from the spruce tree, moose in the willows,
the distant scream of a chainsaw, blade dull,
sawdust smoldering gold on frozen ground.

The first Spring—burning the ditches,
then summer, smell of alfalfa in the fields,
south wind so hot as to tempt the flags to leave
their poles, to give up waving and fly away.

It's a relief to be so far from Heaven, far
from the gates and the tests, from the looking
down and the sitting in judgment, to breathe
together with those who are born and will die.

Raining at the Lake

When we reach the shore, she drops
the kayak. Lifted by the wake
from a passing power boat, it drifts away.

Her face lights up as a child's before the moon.
Waist deep, she falls backward and her wings
disappear. "No water in Heaven," she says.

No ingestion, no excretion, no urination,
no perspiration, no renal failure, no kidneys,
no thirst, no fields to irrigate or toilets to flush.

She fills her cap and pours the water over
her head, cups her hands to drink. "No, no!"
I shout. "Giardia—it gives you diarrhea."

Filling the cap again, she pours it down
the front of her t-shirt. I look away but
too slowly and she catches my eye.

Paddling like a dog, she grabs the boat
and climbs in. The first drops of rain fall,
Khah, khah, khah, the gulls call.

First Date

There was what her father told her
and what her mother told her,
what her mother told her father
to tell her, and what her older sister
told her. Her older brother kept
his mouth shut. It's odd being
the youngest, babied and ignored.

And how did everyone at school
know about it as if the student body
were an actual body breathing hard,
no one sure whether to dress up
like cheerleaders and do cartwheels
across the grass, or play coach—
the pregame pep talk, down by ten
at the half, hang tight, you know
what to do, you've practiced it
a million times, just execute
and we can still pull this one out.

An older girl stops her in the hall,
hand on her arm, skin warm, dry.
It's the girl everyone says did it
before anyone else, who got
pregnant and had an abortion
without telling her boyfriend.

"He was a good boyfriend,"
she says, "sweet. I was the one
who suggested we do it. And he
was careful about precautions,
but nothing's a hundred percent."

She puts the angel's hand
on her belly, moves it in a circle
as if this means something.

It's a first date, the angel
wants to say, that's all.

The Test

The test's at eleven and it's already nine. She sits
on the library steps pouring over the Pentateuch,
as the blood of the lamb pours over the earth.

The stone lions roar, the sudden intake of breath
from Adam and Eve. No point hiding, once
you open your eyes, you're condemned to see.

Better to study math—sine and cosine,
natural numbers, imaginary numbers,
numerators, denominators, square roots.

Or she could stay in bed with her boyfriend.
Casual about preparing, he never worries.
Why should he? She gives him the answers.

What if it's we who must judge the rightness
of our acts? Heaven forbid such thought given
the history of rebellion. Just answer the question.

She closes the book, opens it, closes it again,
stands, smooths her skirt, and goes inside.
Really, there's no point in putting things off.

True or false, multiple choice, fill in the blank.
The afternoon sun heats the room. She lays
her head down on the desk to rest and wham

a songbird slams into the window and slides
to the ground where it lies unmoving, notice
given that the test is over or is about to begin.

Wings

Sometimes it's tricky—

the changing room at the YMCA.
Best to go on Sunday morning when people
are sleeping off Saturday night.

The motorcycle rally in the Black Hills.
Chrome too hot to touch,
don't even consider wearing a bikini.

Winter nights in the neighbors' sauna.
They think she's shy about being naked,
wrapped in a towel.

The yearly medical exam.
The doctor pressing his stethoscope
against her back, listening to her lungs.

It's easier going alone to a concert, the darkened hall,
the dentist noticing nothing but her mouth,
the school plays, all eyes on the kids.

Coats, hoods, capes, sweaters, and scarves
minimize the hump. What'd'ya think
happened to her, people ask.

"Nothing," she says, "happened,"
unwrapping the layers,
feathers shifting in anticipation.

Dinosaurs

You're so lucky, people tell her, able to fly.
The dreamy look in their eyes. But really,
what she likes is driving. When a highway
patrolman pulls her over, she has to admit
she has no license. "Sorry, officer" is all
she can think to say, hoping for the best.

Used to be you said, "I'm an angel" and people
fell to their knees. Now they look at you
like you're a lunatic, or as the righteous say,
a person experiencing symptoms of lunacy.
Nobody believes you. "Sure, you're an angel,
and me, I'm Mary, soon-to-be mother of God."

So many good reasons the age of the automobile
is coming to its end. She'll miss it—her 1950
MG TD, open top two-seater, barely enough room
behind for an overnight bag or a few groceries.
But to drive—midsummer, the winding two-lane
roads in the woods, late afternoon light slanting
through the trees, Dog on the seat next to her,
fur lifted in the wind, ears flapping. They stop
for ice cream—a single scoop—and Dog leans
close for a lick. She whistles and the neighborhood
animals jump in—Coyote, Cat, Ferret, Squirrel,
Skunk. Crow falls from the sky to her shoulder,
chattering some lunatic—oops—story about how
to trick a gull out of a clam or how to steal fire
from the sun. Crow never worries about the future,
says the past's gone, every day's today, waiting
to be made. It's an appealing notion for a spirit
pinned to the wall by the arrow of time. Crow
could care less about time or the MG, defecating
on the red leather seats, red reminding her how
many beings have given their lives for the pleasure

of the open road, animals crushed under the wheels
or smashed like bugs on the windshield. They are
bugs. Not to mention dinosaurs turned to petroleum.

But Crow is no moralist and isn't really saying
anything about dead animals or fossil fuels.
It's the angel, too aware of the world's cruelty
for her own good, paralyzed when a semi collides
with a great blue heron, wings shoveling backwards
to scoop up air, legs broken on the windshield.

She tells Crow to fasten the seatbelt. Seatbelt,
shmeatbelt, you can be careful when you're dead,
hopping from the seat to the dashboard, beak pressed
to the window, scratching vulgarities in the glass,
sidestepping along the angel's shoulder to her ear,
another lunatic squawk, Crow's version of a come-on,
nipping her earlobe as they lean into the turn and hit
the straightaway, front wheels lifting off the ground.

At the Movies

Sitting in the dark eating popcorn drenched
in artificial butter, it's hard to ignore the man
next to her repeating, "I love you. I love you."

Two rows back Mr. and Mrs. Death are writhing
in their seats oblivious to such declarations of love,
the celluloid prelude to the comedy of copulation.

"Psst," Mr. Death hisses, leaning across the seats.
"You keep watching, won't bother us." "Not at all,"
Mrs. Death adds. "We do this six hundred times a day."

It's noon onscreen. A woman crosses the street
surrounded by motorcyclists, engines sweating
in the heat, oily rings staining softening asphalt.

Bored by contrivance, Mr. and Mrs. Death lie
in the aisle, counting—five hundred and one,
five hundred and two, five hundred and three.

At six hundred the motorcyclists stop gunning
their engines and the couple lurch and fall back
as if even they might one day grow tired.

When the man turns and reaches for her hand,
the angel rises, wings tense in the trembling air,
bare feet pulling away from the sticky floor.

Dancing

She knows a little piano bar
where people come to sing and dance
to old swing.

And there's a club downtown with salsa on Thursdays,
an older Latino DJ who loves even the pretentious bastard
who asked if she danced on the one or the two.

Out by the lake there's Cajun on Saturdays.
For twenty years, the same fabulous singer accordionist—
now dead.

For someone for whom
time doesn't matter,
she hates its passing.

It's not how I'd have arranged it,
she whispers to her partner,
a beginner trying hard.

Even Jesus, in Gethsemane, anticipating arrest
the night before his death, called us to form a circle and hold hands.
The universe, he said, belongs to those who dance.
Those who don't will never know what little hold death need have.

The zydeco king, Clifton Chenier,
said, "A person who can dance
can dance to spoons on a cardboard box."
And there's that Brazilian song
about anyone who doesn't like samba
being no good in the head or sick in the feet—
Quem não gosta de samba, bom sujeito não é.
É ruim da cabeça ou doente do pé.

"I'm sorry but I don't speak Portuguese,"
her partner says, then, "I know I'm not very good."

She smiles, pulling him closer.

Tango Shmango

It's feels false to her, the florid sentimentality.
But she likes how the music makes fun of itself.
That's what she thought until a tango musician,
growling like a bear, pulled a knife on her.
And while she couldn't repress a smile, at least
she didn't laugh. When he lunged, she wondered,
not for the first time, why she'd volunteered
for this backwater most see as one step from Hell.

Longtime partner to the inevitable, she spends
her days comforting the dying. Alone after work,
flipping the pages of a magazine or doing dishes,
she tries to imagine it—particles scattering, gone.
She's read that the best drug and alcohol counselors
are often addicts. Surely the same must be true
of bereavement—best done by a human being,
sympathy made real by knowing what's to come.

She leaves the apartment, no hat, coat, or gloves
even as it starts to snow. She haunts pawn shops,
finds a hand-crank gramophone, a stack of 78rpm
records still in their paper sleeves—Aníbal Troilo's
"Pájaro ciego," the blind bird in a golden cage,
Carlos Gardel's "Volver." The famously dead
tango players she's never heard of. Buying nothing,
she leaves the shop and walks to the train station,
stamping her feet and blowing on her hands, snow
coming down harder now, travelers crowding
onto the platforms, hurrying to departing trains,
certain where they're going, when they'll return.

White epaulets appear on the dark shoulders
of the musicians' suits, officers in an army
on the way to losing its war. Maybe I was

wrong, she thinks, I mean what can an angel
know of human life? Not much, she whispers,
bending to wipe snow from their shoes, glossy
black coffins disappearing into the earth.

At the Museum

Lot, having escaped the sins of Sodom
in the painting by Peter Paul Rubens,
is holed up in a cave with his daughters
who give him cup after cup of wine.
Blind drunk, he sleeps with the elder
on the first night and the younger
on the next and both end up pregnant.
To save humanity, they explain.

Jan Brueghel the elder paints Noah herding
a confused mass of animals toward the ark
beached at low tide in the distance, never mind
the limited space on a forty-cubit wooden boat,
and never mind the mosquitos buzzing in the dark
below decks, the female puncturing the skin
of the other animals, sucking their blood,
the black widow spider eating her mate as they
copulate. Widow, mother, daughter, sister, wife,
the woman always gets the bad rap. If the Lord's
really a man, the angel thinks, he's a dick.

In *The Sacrifice of Abraham*, Rembrandt ignores
the climb up the hill, the Lord commanding
the father to burn his son who carries the wood
for the fire on which he will die. The angel
delivering a last-minute reprieve grabs Abraham's
wrist and yanks it so his hand opens and the knife
he holds falls though his left hand is still clamped
over his son's face, driving the young man's head
down. The Lord, as invisible as the mosquitos
on the ark, praises obedience as if a man is to be
measured by the length of his childhood
and a story by the number of times it's told.

Raphael in *St. Michael Vanquishing Satan*
paints the archangel hovering above the prince
of darkness, one foot on his back, spear
poised to be driven into the evil one's head.
Sometimes Michael stands on Satan's head
pressing his face into the dust. Sometimes
the spear is a dagger, a golden sword,
the flaming tail of a comet driven into
Satan's ribcage or cutting off his head.

Does art breed cruelty, she wonders, or simply
reflect it, the smell of linseed oil, the grinding
of pigments and the preparation of the canvas.
The painter's apprentice, a sweet young man,
stares shyly at the angel's back, the prominent
hump where her wings have been bound.

Job's Lawsuit

When the Lord gavels the proceedings
into being, Job struggles to stand, barely
manages to whisper his name. His lawyer
is the angel. That's a good sign but the Lord,
defendant in the case, has appointed himself
judge, jury, expert witness, bailiff, and court
reporter. He bangs the gavel again, says,
"Court is now in session." The angel calls
her first and only witness, the Lord.

A swirling fills the courtroom. "But this
is a whirlwind," the angel cries. "It could be
anyone." "The witness may dress as he likes,"
the judge responds. "Make your case." "Yes,
Your Honor." She waves a piece of paper.
"This deposition attests to a wager Mr. Ha-Satan
made with the defendant." "The court accepts
no depositions." She turns to the whirlwind.
"Did you accept this wager?" No answer.
Someone in the gallery coughs. Dust falls
on the angel's yellow pad, obscuring her notes.
She wipes her eyes. Struggling to keep up,
the air conditioner smells of burning plastic.

"Perhaps I should address you as Mr. Elohim,
another name you're known by, is it not?"
"Objection. Counsel implies based on supposition."
"Sustained." "Did you on October tenth speak
with Mr. Ha-Satan?" Still no answer. "Did you
accept his offer to destroy my client's flocks,
houses, barns, fences, household furnishings,
handmade clothing, cutlery, and irreplaceable
mementos both silver and bronze?" The wind
picks up forming one of those tiny tornados
people call dust devils. "Near Christmas

did you again speak with Mr. Ha-Satan,
this time in Chaldea where he was convicted
of vagrancy? I remind you that you are under
oath." "Objection. Irrelevant and prejudicial."
"Sustained." Which way to turn? "I have
here a photo of Mr. Ha-Satan strolling about
the earth as he pleases. Shortly after this photo
was taken, he disappeared and my client
was beset with pox, boils, and phlebitis."
"Objection." "Sustained." Of course
it's sustained. Why try? It's a kangaroo
court, the deck is stacked, the fix is in.

She can only believe the great arc of history
turns toward justice, and so goes on.
"You accepted a second wager to murder
my client's field workers and herders
along with vast numbers of camel, oxen,
donkey, and sheep. You agreed to murder
my client's three daughters and seven sons."
"I gave him new children." His first words.
Even the air conditioner whirs to a halt.

"Members of the jury will wipe this statement
from their minds," the judge orders. Trembling,
the angel spreads her wings and hovers above
the courtroom. "Genocide, Holocaust, Shoah."
"Objection." Of course objection—objection,
objection, objection. She shuffles her papers,
requests a recess, considers a plea bargain.

The Prostitute

Her hair is cut short
and left tousled
suggesting innocence
but it's only practical
given how many times
a day she has to shampoo it.

Some men can't do it
with her. They say her heart
is warm, that she understands
sorrow and vulnerability
but she reminds them
of their mothers or sisters.

Too easy to confuse her
with the therapist angel
or the Virgin Mother.

It gives them pause.
Without complaining exactly,
they ask for someone else.

As for her employer,
it's no different
from the law or dentistry—
you can't be the one
clients turn down
too often.

The fact that some like her
only makes matters worse,
coming again and again.

Academy Award

A little chagrined to have played
herself and kept secret how she's
a real angel, agreeing to wear
the lowcut dress and high heels
while running across the rain-soaked
roof of an airport parking garage
pursued by a Colombian drug dealer.

Hard to know what the Lord intends
given how fast the scenes change
and how bad the movie is—no
Song of Bernadette or *Joan of Arc.*
Too late for second thoughts now.
From here on out it's endless
car chases and burning buildings,
hardball talk from cynical cops
and worldly priests, chalk outlines
on the sidewalks where the bodies
had lain, sirens, screams, and mounds
of money drenched in blood.

After so long a nameless extra,
one of the infinite arrows of God,
to be Best Actress, lonely winner
among the jostling aspirants, stone
of envy thrown and sinking now
into the lake of longing.

Atomic Bomb

Pulling off the welding goggles the scientists
gave her to wear during the test, she's surprised
to see the men jumping up and down, hugging
each other, Rabi demanding ten dollars from
Oppenheimer—a bet about the size of the blast.

A bottle of whisky is going the rounds—drink up,
it worked, the sand floor of the valley called
Journey of Death now green glass as if some
second creator showed up thumbing his nose
at the simpleton who made the first world, wind
carrying a thirty-mile-wide wave of radiation
ninety miles northeast, birds beating against it,
fallout landing on the backs of cows and goats,
cats and dogs, the housetops of ranchers inside.

"How do you feel?" she asks the man passing
her the bottle. Jubilant. Surprised. Relieved.
Elated. But it doesn't last long. These men
who made the bomb may be slightly drunk
but they're not stupid. It's already catching up
to them—a goat bleeding from the mouth,
a cow from the anus, the family border collie
losing its hair, and the cat clawing at its skin.

Oppenheimer quotes the *Bhagavad Gita*—
"Now I am become Death, destroyer of worlds."
Bainbridge calls it, "A foul and awesome display . . .
Now we are all sons of bitches." They cling to now
as if the future can be told to wait forever just around
the corner. When the bottle reaches her again, she drinks,
asks the man who handed it to her, "What's your name?"
tempted to stroke his hair, comfort him, forgive him,
even as she wants to slap him silly.

Show and Tell

On Tuesday morning a child takes the angel
to school for show and tell. The poor kid
was so embarrassed the week before when
she took a rock she'd found at the creek,
glowing as a tiny sun. At school, it became
a dull gray thing and the class laughed.

Not this week. Wait'll they see the angel,
the answer to the conundrum about how
we can know a particle's position or its
velocity but not both at once, a problem
not addressed in the second grade when
some kids have trouble using scissors
and a fair number still can't read.

The angel is like the water in the creek
flowing over and around whatever's
in the way. Sometimes when her day
has been especially hard, the child goes
there after school and sits watching
the light and the water dancing.
That's how she sees it.

When the teacher calls on her, she stands
and, with the angel's hand in hers, walks
to the front of the classroom where she
waits while two of her classmates finish
cleaning the blackboard, removing the ten
new spelling words, slapping the erasers
together, chalk dust hanging in the air.

At seven, she already knows the looks,
the doubt in their eyes, the sneers from
the mean kids, the gray rock in their minds.
Come on, this is no angel. It's probably

just your Aunt María in a white dress
with wings she bought at the costume store.

When the laughter starts again, the angel
does nothing, doesn't flap her wings
or start to glow or tell them to shut up.
But she gives the child's hand a squeeze
as the two walk together back to her desk.

Call Him If You Want

She finds herself humming the old song—
call him up and tell him what you want.
There's a phone booth on the corner
where yesterday was only a trash can.
If you're sick and you want to get well,
tell him what you want. The line ain't
never busy. Tell him what you want.

Dropping a handful of quarters in the slot
she dials her parish priest. How fine to hear
his voice, but wait, it's a recording—due to
increased call volume and the ongoing effects
of the COVID-19 global pandemic we are
experiencing longer than usual wait times.

She can see her face in the glass—the humble
angel—bullshit—implacability as great as
the Lord's. Childhood prayers—now I lay me
down to sleep. Dropping another quarter
in the slot she sets the receiver down, gathers
paper and rags and a packing crate she found
in the alley to start a fire, the phone booth
a damaged space capsule drifting ever farther
into emptiness, her suit too thin to keep her
from freezing, oxygen almost gone. She checks
the line and steps back to warm herself by the fire.
God only knows how long she'll be on hold.

Gettysburg

How close she came to revealing herself,
swooping down on the now-former president
to seal his mouth. His words—I was elected
in a landslide, greatest landslide in history,
more people at my inauguration than ever
before. If my election was a woman, she'd be
a ten. My daughter is so hot. If I wasn't her
father. Not all women are tens—maybe you
have to settle for a five, even a three. Sad.
Some people hate this country I'm making
great again, bad people who hate the good
people who voted for me. A lot of men died
here, some good, some bad, three thousand,
maybe five. They're finding more bodies
every day. Kids in school should be taught
the American heroes. Teachers give tests.
Who needs it? Life's a test. I don't have to
tell you. Nobody won more primaries than me.
He pauses, eyes pinned to the angel's chest.
Really, she should have shut him up, but all
she wanted was to sit quietly and mourn those
who gave their lives. Now, afraid she'll vomit,
she stands and moves down the aisle. "Sorry,"
she says, "it's so hot." And humid. The flags
hang limp on their poles, soldiers leaning on
their shovels. "Beautiful," the former president
says as the angel turns, tempted again to betray
her vow of noninterference, the same vow
she took to play the emotionally cool Vulcan
on the *Star Trek* television show, hurtling
through space each week in search of new
worlds. Would it have been so bad to have
landed and struck him dumb, to have left
each new planet a little better than it was?

Hitchhiking with Jesus

"I'll stay here at the edge of the road
behind this hawthorn," Jesus says.
"People are way more likely to pick up
a woman on her own. When someone stops,
open the door but don't get in till I come out."

They're on their way to India not long
after Jesus brought a widow's son back
from the dead. These miracles always
make him dizzy, nauseous, afraid
he's going to throw up.

"I figure if I can take the pain away,
I should, not so much for the dead
as for the living, another wailing
mother fallen to the ground, fists
pounding away like it was the earth's
fault, dust rising. I know it's wrong
to defy the laws of nature but I had
to do something, don't you think?"

She wants to say no, if you create
mortality, you have to stand by it
but she says nothing, waggles her
thumb aimed down the highway.

"So I put my hand on her shoulder,
told her I'd bring him back. 'Get up,'
I said to the kid. Nothing happens.
I wait a minute and try again, 'Get up.'
I could hear the murmur from the crowd,
feel the pickpockets and prostitutes
drifting closer, casual like they were
on holiday, water sellers packing up
for the day, hustlers calling out odds—

seven to four the dead man stays dead,
five to three, two to one. The doubt
had started rising with the dust,
the woman still pounding away.
Really, I couldn't take it. Someone
grabbed my sleeve. I pulled away
and slapped the kid—not hard—just
to get his attention. One last time,
'Get up,' and in a whisper, 'please.'
With that, he lurched into my arms,
coughed, and blinked furiously.
It was like everyone inhaled at once
and there in the silence the only
sound was the buzzing of the flies."

You'd think if you had this power,
you'd feel good, but look at him
hiding there in the hawthorn, the sun
beating down on the empty highway,
the clouds piling up, a storm on the way.

She ought to tell him the first car won't
be here for nearly two thousand years,
that he'd be better off living in the world
as it is, that if they pooled their cash,
they could take the bus.

At the Hardware Store

Even in Heaven the house needs to be repainted
every ten years or so and who's going to do it
but the angel. Alone on a ladder, she starts—
power wash, scrape, fill cracks and holes, replace
rotten boards. Then the hardware store, comparing
paint chips—the range of blues, reds, and greens,
the more daring mango, reminiscent of the Garden
before all was lost, pine needles softening the ground,
paddling a kayak across the estuary, tide coming in,
sun slicing through the mangroves, sliced papaya
on a plate to eat on the porch, too hot inside, kids
kicking a soccer ball in the road, dried palm fronds
burning. A warm night lying beneath the stars,
cows crossing the pasture, bells ringing, the earth
spinning on its axis making her dizzy when she stands.

"Ma'am?" the clerk asks, thinking how far away
she seems. Repeats, "Ma'am, that mango's beautiful
but it fades awful fast." So much fades awful fast—
a day gone in the blink of an eye, a week, a month,
a millennium. All the people she's seen born and died,
and how few she can remember. Something as simple
as a mother's and a father's name, their children's
names. There was a picnic she remembers—chicken
with potato salad laid out in bowls on a blanket spread
on the ground, a lake, blue sky, birds singing, kids
splashing around in the water, but the names, what
were they? "Ma'am," the clerk tries for the third time.

It's not just the paint but the rags and drop clothes,
the brushes and thinner. The house should look good
no matter the worn-out furniture and ancient plumbing,
the past owners. She holds the paint chips by the window,

focusing not on eternity or an all-powerful, all benevolent
first carpenter, but on the house that needs to be painted,
how the color will look in sunlight, how fast it will fade.

Potluck

The paper stapled to the light pole reads, *Potluck*
Supper in Church Hall following Sunday Service.
It's mimeographed and there's a blue smear
where someone grabbed it before the ink was dry.
"No way," the angel says. "A potluck in Heaven?
And mimeograph—no one's used that for eons."

In her day everyone was Catholic—spaghetti
and garlic bread after Mass, a creole band—
accordion and rubboard. Now the Lutherans
bring tuna hot dish in the back of hybrid SUVs.
The Baptists make white bread sandwiches
with miracle whip, coleslaw, and potato chips.
The Unitarians smile at everyone, passing
around grilled tofu on a bed of mixed greens.

The same flyer announces the same potluck
on every light pole on the block stretching
as far as the eye can see—horizon line,
smell of creosote, the angel, stapler in hand,
quickstepping pole after pole into eternity.

III.

THE

POET

The Doorbell

The doorbell rings. It's the angel,
no dramatic plummeting from the clouds.
She comes up the steps as ordinary as the mailman
on a winter day handing me a catalogue
for warm clothes and one of the endless flyers
offering a good price on hearing aids.
"What is it?" I ask. "Has someone died?"

"Of course someone's died. But no, it's not that."
She shuffles as if to scrape the mud off her shoes.
"I'd rather you didn't put words in my mouth.
That's all." Then turns and walks away,
the mailman heading back to his truck.

It's not me, I call after her, it's the poet.
We're not the same person, you know.
But she's gone. I turn and press the doorbell.
It's true the ringing seems awfully faint
as if it were coming from across the street
or from the TV in the basement.
I have to listen hard, leaning on the bell,
admiring how she got right to the point,
how quickly she turned to leave.

Repainting the House

"What the hell'd'ya think
you're doing?" my father asks,
waving a book in my face,
his finger pressed to my name
on the spine. First time
I've seen him in eight years.
"So now you're a poet.
How much they pay you
for that?"

Scraping the flaking paint
off the wall in the alley,
I say, "This blue's held up
pretty well."

He looks at me
as if for the first time.

I put the scraper down
and pick up the steel brush.
With house painting
prep is the key.
Anyway, I like to work
with my hands.

Now he rubs his palm
across the cover,
not so much a caress
as sanding the edges
on a rough-cut board.

Opening the new can
of blue, I wonder where
he found this book,

but don't ask.
With my father
and with poetry too,
the less said the better.

Reading the Odyssey at the Kitchen Table

The story's tragic but I go on turning
the pages—the ten-year journey
in wooden boats, Odysseus wandering
the seas, son Telemachus growing up,
wife Penelope beset by lecherous suitors,
the multitudinous gods crossing the sky.

It seems they're always hiding something—
these gods—papering over their mistakes,
the gods who came before.

Physicists claim matter is mostly
empty space. I slap the table
and my hand stings. So much for physics.

"Do you remember the day our father died,"
my sister asks me, "the sun beating down
burning him up from the inside out?"
I remember the rain and birds, his head
on the pillow, how wispy his hair was,
the shame I felt, feeling no loss.

Passing the cliffs where the Sirens sing
the sailors shove wax into their ears,
but Odysseus would listen, makes them
tie him to the mast, the crackle of paper
as I turn the page to hear their song.

Day after day Penelope sews a bedspread
knowing that when she finishes, she must
choose a bridegroom, the suitors eating up
her husband's wealth. Each night, betting
on his return, she undoes what she's done.
It feels right to sew truth from the fabric

of fiction, the woman here in the flickering
candlelight unraveling the stitches, Odysseus
clinging to a plank, me hoping not loving
your father is not the same as killing him.

A Poem with a Wall

Two New England farmers are repairing
the stone wall dividing one's apple orchard
from the other's pine trees. One says,
"Before I built a wall I'd ask to know
what I was walling in or walling out."
The other, "Good fences make good neighbors."

It's not as if it's a real wall, after all,
though there are those who bawl
we need a real wall thick and tall
to keep out aliens who come to call.

But the alien ship is an intergalactic one
powered by accelerating time and metered rhyme.
No wall will stop it even battered by its passage
through worm holes and along string lines,
squeezing from one universe to the next,
each lying atop the other like the pages
in a yellow legal pad, a deposition
taken at an asylum hearing.

Near sunset I stroll through my Arizona
neighborhood within sight of the wall.
I can hear a bird singing on the other side,
the New England farmers two thousand
miles away stacking stone upon stone.

The Eye of the Blackbird

"Among twenty snowy mountains,
The only moving thing
Was the eye of the blackbird."

That's the beginning
of the first poem I read
on my own, the first poem I loved.

Excited, I drew the scene—the blackbird's head,
the moving eye, the snowy mountains—
and tacked it to the wall above my bed.

Maybe it was being
a child of the desert
who'd never seen snow,

or that there were no books in our house
aside from the *Encyclopedia Britannica*
purchased at the grocery with Green Stamps,

or the contrast—the world offered
to me by the poet more beautiful
than the one in which I lived,

for mine was not a beautiful world,
filled as it was with threats and blows,
and nothing made clear.

The years pass—the moving eye,
the snowy mountains, the child in me
reading again for the first time.

A Little More Beautiful

My grandfather became something of a poet
because of the war—the shelters and the waiting,
the rocket attacks followed by silence.
He said the night seemed darker,
and that this suggested the power of fear
or the absence of streetlamps.

My mother, nine, went room to room
sealing the blackout curtains, serious
about letting no light escape.

Called up and unable to promise he'd return,
he wrote a poem for his wife, my grandmother,
the only poem he ever wrote,
which he showed me after her death—

> Every year
> we get
> a little more
> beautiful.

"Awfully short," I said. "Yes," he answered,
"there wasn't much time."

Getting Some Fun Out of Life

My father, one of the unhappiest men
I've known, loved the music of Billie Holiday,
especially "Getting Some Fun Out of Life,"
which I remember him singing when
he thought no one was there.

When we want to love, we love.
When we want to kiss, we kiss.
With a little petting we're getting
some fun out of life.

Once looking through the tools
in my father's shop, I found a paperback
novel, the kind my mother would never
let me read. Goddammit, my father said,
raging in pursuit of the fun he never got.

It's spring, the scent of blossoms in the air,
my father running for the bus to work
at the extrusion mill. Goddammit again.

Not long before his death he took me to a party
at the rec center in the senior housing complex
where he and my mother lived. He had a new
thermos filled with vodka and orange juice.

I'd never seen either of my parents drink
and knew that my mother thought it a sin.
My father laughed, slapping me on the back.

After his death I asked my mother why
she married him. "I felt sorry for him,"
she said. And why she stayed married?
"You make your bed, and you lie in it."

My father's longing, my mother's regret.
How easy it is here at my desk, writing
these poems, getting some fun out of life.

Loving Poetry

My wife loves this poem,
loves it so much she's hugging me.
I told this to the editor who rejected it.

"That's just it," he said. "Your wife
loves this poem because she loves you,
not because the poem's any good."

I felt bad but thought,
it's true, my wife loves me
and better her than the editor.

Still, I worked over the poem,
trying to fix it. Finished,
I showed it to my wife.

"What about the ending?" I asked.
"Is the ending okay?" "Okay?"
She said, "It's great. I love it."

Walt Whitman

As the city spilled to the west,
the developers put up more
cinder block houses for the poor
who would be middle class
but the cars were still on blocks
and my father was still taking the bus
to work at the extrusion mill,
battered lunchbox in hand.
Arizona, no union, shit pay.

I imagined myself
the orphan son in a Hollywood movie,
apprenticed as groom to a knight,
but I would be a knight myself,
and asked the princess for a token,
told her I'd enter the lists
and win for her. She, smarter
than her see-through blouse
and my imagination implied,
laughed, said, "You want to win
for yourself, not me.
If you would prove your love,
lose." I said I'd do it
as I wanted to be in the movies
as much as the next guy.
I worked the poem over
but never got the line
breaks right.

Coming home in the afternoon,
lunchbox empty, my father
saw me writing and asked,
"Who do you think you are,
Walt Whitman?"

I was surprised, not so much
that he knew who Whitman was,
but that he knew I did, I do,
think I am, Walt Whitman.

Penultimate Question

I dreamt I gave a poetry reading.

The critics loved it, praising my mastery
of an astonishing array of formal techniques.
I stuck filaments against the firmament
and encouraged stars to tumble down stairs.
My immersions were encased in emulsions,
words flying from my mouth like the shattered
teeth of a boxer on his way to the mat.

I was untroubled by the poet's ultimate question—
to speak or not to speak? I felt good and glad,
like God. Someone in the audience rose
and yelled, "Filament, firmament, stars, stairs,
immersion, emulsion. If the poet's ultimate
question is 'to speak or not to speak,'
the listener's is 'Where's the bathroom?'"

I wanted to ask if my interrogator was a poet
but woke needing to pee and by the time
I got back to bed, I'd forgotten my dream
and had to make this one up.

Talking over Coffee

"It's hard to accept," my friend says, "what's happening
these days. Even this coffee—most people can't
afford it." I look out the window uncertain
about guilt. I like the Northwest—
the rain, the bookstores,
the coffee.

One table over a man and a woman are arguing
about God—not whether he exists
or about her race and gender
but about their cruelty.

"Take the flood," the woman says. "God saves Noah, his family,
and two of every creature including parasitical protozoa
and malarial mosquitos. He drowns the rest of us
including kids holding their pet dogs and cats.
Drowns the pet dogs and cats, too."

"Don't forget the pet guinea pigs and hamsters,"
the man adds, turning to smile at us.

"When people don't know what else to do, they make jokes,"
my friend says, "like this about the flood. But drowning's
not a pleasant way to go." What is, I want to ask,
and how would my friend know, but I keep
my mouth shut and listen.

It's not God who's cruel but we who invented him,
who tied him to a chair, handcuffed and gagged.

"What about pulling the gag out with your feet?"
my friend asks. "You're a writer, aren't you?
Write what you want. Or do you think
a writer's just God without the power
to make anything happen?"

Maybe God's just a writer with nothing
to say, I think, drinking
my coffee.

Splitting Wood

My father won't let up
about my book of poems.

"You really wrote this?"
he asks, shaking it the way
a cat shakes a mouse.

It's unclear what
I'm meant to say.

"Listen to this one."

"It's okay," I say,
"I've read them."

I lift the ax over my head
and bring it down hard,

stunned by the shriek
of cottonwood and pine
coming apart,

the cat toying
with the mouse.

A Peach

In the famous poem
over a hundred years old,
the narrator can't decide
if he should eat a peach.
Do I dare, he asks,
rhyming *peach* with *beach*
and thereby suggesting
that in the end the particular
fruit is of no consequence.

In the more recent famous
poem, the poet's in a car.
"drive, the passenger says, "for
christ's sake, look
out where yr going."

The most famous poet
of all wrote, "I confess
that I have lived."

Poems often have several
subjects as in this one—
history, fame, fresh fruit,
driving, even poetry itself,
which is a very bad subject.

I once read that poets
are failed bandleaders.
and it's true people
mostly prefer songs,
the subject of which
is almost always love
or its absence.

Identity

I might have been anything—a drunk, a drunk driver, throwing up
  drunk, drunk at my own wedding, dead drunk, a drunk dog, a dead
  dog, a deadbeat dad—still drunk.

Or sober—an unwed teenaged girl, pregnant in a state that's banned
  abortion, thrown out of the house and soon to be a single mother
  working two jobs and going to community college part time, I just
  wanta pay the rent and have enough left to get by.

I always wanted to be a veterinarian, or a test pilot but I was color blind.

I could be a mo-fo, maybe not, I can't even say mo-fo with conviction.

Along with life, I'm nonbinary. My neighbor asks if I mean I'm not a
  computer. It's true I'm not a computer and since the non-binary is
  the living, I guess I'm alive.

I'm plagued by the dream of being everything—man, woman, child,
  angel, God, Satan, Black, white, BIPOC, LGBTQ+, Vietnamese,
  Chinese, Basque, Hutu, native, indigenous, mostly Mexican—one
  of those with whom I grew up, truthfully, I want to be the alien
  landing and opening the door to my ship—this is not a kidnapping,
  I'd say, more an invitation.

What about speed freak, cokehead, opium dreamer, LSD researcher,
  seeker through mescalin, peyote, heroin—the real thing, the dark
  tracks, needle marks between my toes, the crossroads where fashion
  and self-destruction meet.

I'm gonna say what I mean, mean what I say, mean something whatever
  that means, be mean.

I might try anorexia, bulimia—finished with those I'd go to dental
  school to fix my teeth.

In the next war, I'll be a draft dodger. As a woman, I support equal rights,
  when they start the draft for women, I'll dodge it in another skin.

I'll be a walk-on for the Dodgers, teach middle school PE with a focus
  on dodge ball, submit an application to read this poem at the
  Geraldine R. Dodge Poetry Festival, not really, no way, no more
  dodging for me.

I'll go from the Dodgers to the Angels, start a church, introduce
  democracy in Heaven, Sunday softball after services, sliding into
  home plate and when the umpire screams, "Out!" I'll be up on the

balls of my feet pumping my fists and screaming, "Are you blind?" knowing there's no arguing with the umpire.

I'm changing the pronoun I use but I'll keep my old pronoun for my mother, I'm inventing a new pronoun, I'm happy to be called any pronoun you like, I am a pronoun, I want you to be happy, I want you to be a pronoun, I want us all to be happy pronouns.

The best is to be a bum—the less we do the less we can ruin. I'll lie around all day singing odes to laziness, one of Matthew's birds of the air who neither sow nor reap and yet the Lord feeds them. I don't know how far I'd trust Matthew given my experience of the world—work, work, work.

I'll be a worker, then—a worker bee, a food-aid worker, do the Lord's work, work like a dog, hey, this generator is broken, it won't work, nothing works, keep working.

Politics, that's the ticket—power and money—but you have to pick an ideology—Democrat, socialist, democratic socialist, Republican, fascist, Nazi, libertarian, anarchist, nihilist, I don't know maybe politics wasn't the best idea I ever had.

I'll make mistakes, apologize for my mistakes, cling to my mistakes, be a mistake.

I'm spiritual—Buddhist, Hindu, Christian, Jew, Muslim, Pantheist—I embrace all faiths and creeds. I'm large. Actually I'm just fat.

I could be a patriarch, but I'd have to be a father, a good father, no deadbeat me, a father figure, I'll have a good figure, I'll figure things out.

Time to go on television—a drag-show host, a drag show contestant, a drag racer, a drag line—a mechanized excavator and crawler—a nine year old taking a drag on my older sister's cigarette.

I'll get a wig, disguise myself, go to Las Vegas to drink in rooftop bars— the Legacy, the Foundation, the Ghostbar, 108 Drinks, the Skyfall Lounge, I'm a drunk again falling from the sky, the ground coming up fast, the poem I call life coming to its inevitable end.

Clinging to Nothing

All my pwoblems, I begin, maybe evwybody's pwoblems,
quoting Spiderman in the poem by Jim Hall, Spiderman
with an odd accent or minor speech impediment, called
by the governor to catch some burglars who are only
trying to rip off color-TV sets. When Spiderman asks
what do I care about color-TV sets, the students laugh.
And when he gathers up his wopes and wittle bundle
of equipment they laugh some more. But when
he complains—nothing big happens, the burglars
keep trying to rip off color-TV sets, the governor
keeps calling—they nod as if they too toss and turn
through the night in the throes of existential ennui.

Once I would have asked how I could see myself
in the daily dilemmas of a comic book hero. Now
I look at my students—high school sophomores
slogging through English class—Romeo and Juliet,
Browning and Keats—and I am in my own cramped
desk with them, no longer an infant, not yet an adult.

I had a recurring dream through childhood and into
middle age: I'm running across a field of grasses
nearly as tall as I am, golden, waving in a light breeze.
A lion, the same golden as the grasses, is chasing me.
I can feel its footsteps in the motion of the earth, hear
its breathing in my lungs, see the glow in its eyes.
I come to a cliff and with nowhere to turn, step over
the edge. I'm falling, arms whirling, legs churning,
the ground coming up fast, clinging to life.

The students waiting for the end of the poem, I leap
into space and fly across town from rooftop to rooftop,
dogs barking in the yards below, forgetting Spiderman
for a moment, tossing away the little bundle of ropes
and equipment tied to my waist, clinging to nothing.

Western History

It's not poetry exactly, the story of Ed Trafton,
last of the Yellowstone highwaymen, how one
summer day in 1914, he stepped into the center
of the road by the bright water of Shoshone Lake
and pulled a black silk neckerchief across his face
as the first of fifteen tourist coaches came in view.
Holding up his hand like the crossing guard
at an elementary school, he said, "Please step
down and drop your valuables on the blanket . . .
take a standing seat and witness the convention."

That's pretty poetic and he might have said it.
But the neckerchief—it was so hot. A tall woman
in a tan suit described Trafton as "rather elegant,
steady and calm with a lovely sense of humor
and a smile that made his watery blue eyes sparkle."
"He was so friendly," another of the victims said.
"We figured it was a set-up." "Polite." "The kind
of man who would have made a good president."

An elderly lady dropped her purse scattering bills,
coins, a comb, a tin of Nivea creme, and a deck
of playing cards in the dust. Trafton bent to pick up
the fallen valuables, said, "Madam, you keep these,
you look as if you need them more than I do."
Holding the last card, the jack of hearts, he added,
"I'll just keep this." The horses stamped their feet
and switched their tails to drive away the flies
and the water, lapping at the shore, promised
nothing bad would happen. Unseen birds sang.

A young couple on their honeymoon wanted a photo
by the blanket. The elderly lady asked if she could
have Ed's neckerchief. The coach driver pulled out
one of the new Brownie cameras and lined everyone

up by the beguiling highwayman, click of the shutter
louder than the cicadas chirring in the dry grass.

It's an appealing story—the long summer afternoon,
the sweet smell of pine resin rising in the heat, watches,
bracelets, and earrings hitting the earth, cash piling up,
the blanket disappearing under the mound of treasure,
the tourists waving goodbye as Trafton touches the lead
horse lightly on the rump to send it on its way. Pulling
the neckerchief up over the bridge of his nose, he steps
again into the road as another coach rounds the bend,
the sun falling behind the hills, the long shadows
of the geysers and the ancient stink of the mudpots,
Shoshone Lake shimmering below the point.

Intruders

I wrote to tell my father I'd been appointed
poet laureate of Wyoming, explaining how
I went to the legislature to address the senators
and representatives, how I'd been charged
with writing poems in moments of historic
significance though such moments were
undefined, how I meant to address big issues—
endangered species, the decline of coal
and economic transition, climate change,
equality before the law, ranked-choice voting,
health care including a woman's right
to an abortion, not that anyone would
make her get one, how after I published
a poem with the F word in it, the governor
put his feet up on his desk and accused me
of poetic mediocrity, asking why he shouldn't
fire me. Then a friend called to say only
a bad poet could be appointed state laureate.
It was surprising—my friend and the governor
on the same page. I wrote my father again,
this time to tell him that mostly I work
with school children, helping them enjoy
reading while policemen in dark uniforms
patrol the halls watching for intruders.

Among the Forgotten Poets

Not the one writing this book
though he too will be forgotten
but the others, the ones found
in the famous bookstore with its
high ceilings and wrap-around
mezzanine, the smell of paper
and polished wood, the forgotten
poets waiting behind their tattered
covers, cheek by jowl with one
another, never to be lonely again.

It was the rain that drove me in—
hair stuck to my scalp, feet soaked.

I walked up and down the aisles,
brushing the books' spines, fingers
trailing across the poets' names.
Closing my eyes I drew one to me,
a poet I'd never heard of who,
in the first poem—"Alcatraz"—
claimed he saw the famous San
Francisco dream while visiting
the city, sitting in a café drinking
coffee and writing. It sounds so
romantic—the city, the solitude,
the expensive coffee, the poet
writing on a napkin or the back
of his hand, maybe about the deep
unconscious sea or Minnesota,
feeling he must rush to his hotel
room to organize his thoughts
into a poem that will never be
forgotten. But few things are
more depressing than an empty
hotel room in the middle of the day.

Coffee finished and rain stopped,
the poet stepped outside and fished
around in his pockets for a coin
he dropped into the Automatic Eye,
one of those pay telescopes found
along the pier. The coin fell into
the slot and the telescope whirred
to life, bringing Alcatraz close.
Looking across the water, the poet
saw a woman with a spyglass
scanning the shoreline, leaning
into this century as if from another
time, an ocean out of which the poem
might be struggling. With her next
sweep across the water, the woman
noticed the poet. Pulling the spyglass
from her eye, she called to a man
standing nearby, a figure I hadn't
noticed before who must have been
there all along—her husband Arthur.
"Art," she called, "there's someone
watching us." "Someone we know?"
"No, I've no idea who it is."

Art Marches On

After my father's death, my mother moved
to a cottage on Cape Cod, far from her son—
me—who remained addled by ambition,
another word for delusional identification
with the self, banging on her door wanting
a loan. "Just to get me by," I said, "till I finish
my novel. No more poems, the novel means
real money but I've got to go deeper, face
the demons and monsters in the human breast,
expose myself to vital harrowing experience
the way the great writers of the past did,
be forged in the fire of war, crime, poverty,
insanity, the peril and dark night of the soul."

"Uh-huh," my mother said, opening the door.
She offered me a toasted cheese sandwich
with tomato and basil, olives, roasted hazelnuts,
and, from the table, a view of the sea,
the eternal waves rolling in as art marches on.

NOTES

Page 15 The phrase "Aita, zer ekarri diguzu?" in "Long Haul" means, "Father, what have you brought us?"

Page 20—"Things to Do in Buffalo, Wyoming, While Waiting Out the Corona Virus" was begun during the global COVID-19 pandemic. From January 2020 to January 2022, 175,000 children had lost a parent or primary caregiver to COVID. It might have been 174,999 or 176,001, reminding us of the saying that the death of a single person is a tragedy while the death of a million is a statistic. Or to put it another way—if you kill one person you're a murderer, if you kill several you're a gangster, if you kill millions you're a hero. One person more or less—who is that person?

Page 38—The Portuguese lyrics mentioned in "Dancing" are from the song "O Samba da Minha Terra," many versions of which can be heard online. Recordings of the music of Clifton Chenier can be found at folkways.si.edu.

Page 40—The songs mentioned in "Tango Shmango" can be heard online by typing into an internet search bar YouTube Carlos Gardel Volver and YouTube Aníbal Troilo Pájaro Ciego.

Page 44—The biblical version of Job's trials are found in Job, one of the books of Ketuvim which is the third part of Tanakh, the Holy Scriptures as translated for publication by the Jewish Publication Society.

Page 47—Jennifer Jones received the 1944 Academy Award for Best Actress in a Leading Role for her performance in *The Song of Bernadette*. The film was nominated for five Academy Awards. *Joan of Arc* received eight Academy Award nominations including that of Ingrid Bergman for Best Actress. While Bergman did not receive the Oscar, the poem "Academy Award" must not be taken as evidence that she sank into the lake of longing.

Page 48—"Atomic Bomb" reimagines the scene immediately following the explosion of the first nuclear weapon on July 16, 1945, south of Los Alamos, New Mexico, on the plains of the Alamogordo Bombing Range, known as the Jornada del Muerto—the Journey of Death—or maybe the Day Labor of Death. Rabi is Isidor Isaac Rabi, Oppenheimer is J. Robert Oppenheimer, and Bainbridge is Kenneth Tompkins Bainbridge. All three worked on the development of the atomic bomb as physicists with the Manhattan Project, of which Bainbridge was the director.

Page 51—The old song the angel hums in "Call Him If You Want" is "Jesus on the Mainline," sometimes known as "Call Him Up." Two versions can be heard online by typing into an internet search bar YouTube Jesus on the Mainline Ry Cooder and YouTube The Mississippi Mass Choir—Call Him Up.

Page 53—The story told in "Hitchhiking with Jesus" of a widow's son being brought back from the dead appears in the Christian Bible's Gospel of Luke (Luke 7: 11–17).

Page 66—"A Poem With a Wall" is in response to Robert Frost's poem "Mending Wall."

Page 67—"The Eye of the Blackbird" remembers discovering "Thirteen Ways of Looking at a Blackbird" by Wallace Stevens and, with it, discovering poetry.

Page 69—To hear "Getting Some Fun Out of Life," type into an internet search bar YouTube Getting Some Fun Out of Life Billie Holiday.

Page 72—The Hollywood movie mentioned in "Walt Whitman" is *A Knight's Tale*.

Page 78—"A Peach" addresses the narrator in T. S. Eliot's "The Love Song of J. Alfred Prufrock," who after much dithering comes late in life to asking if he might dare to eat a peach. The more recent famous poem is "I Know a Man" by Robert Creeley. The most famous poet is Pablo Neruda, whose memoir is called *Confieso que he vivido*—*I Confess that I Have Lived*. "Poets are bandleaders who have failed" is from Ayi Kwei Armah's *The Beautyful Ones Are Not Yet Born* and appears as the epigraph to *African Rhythm and African Sensibility* by John Miller Chernoff.

Page 81—"Clinging to Nothing" derives from my teaching of Jim W. Hall's "Maybe Dats Your Pwoblem Too." Hall's version of the superhero with a problem predates the troubled Hollywood movie character by many years.

Page 82—The last stagecoach robbery in Yellowstone National Park was carried out by Ed Trafton—the Happy Highwayman—who, on July 29, 1914, held up eighty-two passengers traveling on fifteen stagecoaches. Trafton's serial hold ups occurred at an overlook near Shoshone Lake between Old Faithful and Yellowstone Lake.

Page 85—The poem "Alcatraz" was written by John Engman and appears in his first and only book published in his lifetime *Keeping Still, Mountain* (1983). Engman died in 1996 at age forty-seven, shortly before his second book, *Temporary Help* (1998), appeared. John was my classmate and friend at the Iowa Writers' Workshop. I hope that he and his poems will not be forgotten.